D0509600

Dear Parent:
Your child's love of reading ...

Every child learns to read in a different way and at his or her own speed. Some go back and forth between reading levels and read favourite books again and again. Others read through each level in order. You can help your young reader improve and become more confident by encouraging his or her own interests and abilities. From books your child reads with you to the first books he or she reads alone, there are I Can Read Books for every stage of reading:

SHARED READING
Basic language, word repetition, and whimsical illustrations, ideal for sharing with your emergent reader

BEGINNING READING
Short sentences, familiar words, and simple concepts for children eager to read on their own

READING WITH HELP
Engaging stories, longer sentences, and language play for developing readers

READING ALONE
Complex plots, challenging vocabulary, and high-interest topics for the independent reader

ADVANCED READING
Short paragraphs, chapters, and exciting themes for the perfect bridge to chapter books

I Can Read Books have introduced children to the joy of reading since 1957. Featuring award-winning authors and illustrators and a fabulous cast of beloved characters, I Can Read Books set the standard for beginning readers.

A lifetime of discovery begins with the magical words "I Can Read!"

I Can Read!

READING
2
WITH HELP

SPIDER-MAN 3

SPIDER-MAN
VERSUS
SANDMAN

Adapted by Harry Lime
Illustrated by Steven E. Gordon
Based on the Marvel Comic book by Stan Lee and Steve Ditko
Screenplay by Alvin Sargent
Screen Story by Sam Raimi & Ivan Raimi

HarperCollins *Children's Books*

COLUMBIA PICTURES PRESENTS A MARVEL STUDIOS / LAURA ZISKIN PRODUCTION A SAM RAIMI FILM TOBEY MAGUIRE 'SPIDER-MAN 3' KIRSTEN DUNST JAMES FRANCO THOMAS HADEN CHURCH
TOPHER GRACE BRYCE DALLAS HOWARD THEMES BY DANNY ELFMAN SCORE BY CHRISTOPHER YOUNG EXECUTIVE STAN LEE KEVIN FEIGE JOSEPH M. CARACCIOLO BASED ON THE MARVEL STAN LEE AND STEVE DITKO
PRODUCERS COMIC BOOK BY
MARVEL SPIDER-MAN CHARACTER SCREEN SAM RAIMI & IVAN RAIMI SCREENPLAY ALVIN SARGENT PRODUCED LAURA ZISKIN AVI ARAD GRANT CURTIS DIRECTED SAM RAIMI COLUMBIA
TM & © 2006 MARVEL CHARACTERS, INC. STORY BY BY BY BY PICTURES
ALL RIGHTS RESERVED.
© 2006 COLUMBIA PICTURES INDUSTRIES, INC. ALL RIGHTS RESERVED.
sony.com/Spider-Man

SPIDER-MAN 3

Today is Spider-Man's big day.
Everyone is here to thank a hero,
Spider-Man.

That's me.

Most of the time I am Peter Parker,

just a regular guy.

But today I am Spider-Man.

It looks like the whole city is here.

Old people, young people.

Nice people.

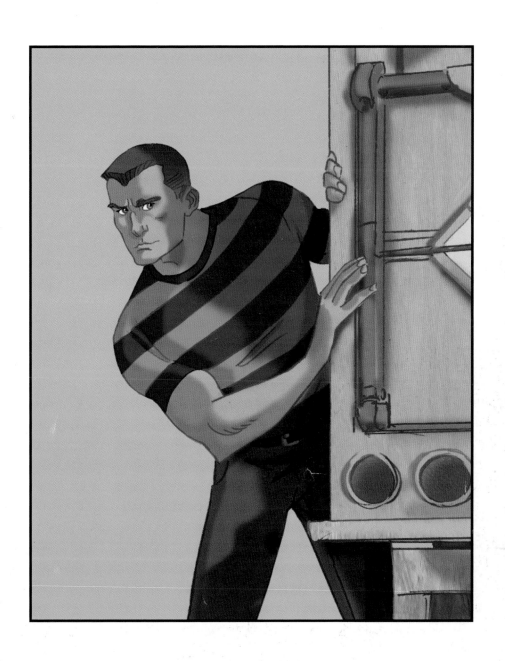

And some not very nice people, too.

I can see Sandman with

my Spidey sense.

He is about to make some trouble.

I always liked playing in the sand
when I was a kid.
But I don't like Sandman.

Sandman is huge.

If I don't stop him,

some of these people will get hurt.

That truck is full of money.

The driver is bringing it to the bank.

It looks like Sandman wants

to withdraw some money right now.

But the money doesn't belong to him.

I have to stop him!

It's time for me to go to work.

I cannot enjoy my party

if a bad guy is planning a crime.

Sandman is stealing
other people's money.

Most of the time,

when I fight bad guys, they give up.

But Sandman is a tricky guy!

First Sandman turns into sand.

Then Sandman jumps into the truck and takes off.

I think I'll go along for the ride.

Sandman may be made of sand,
but he punches very hard!
That hurt!

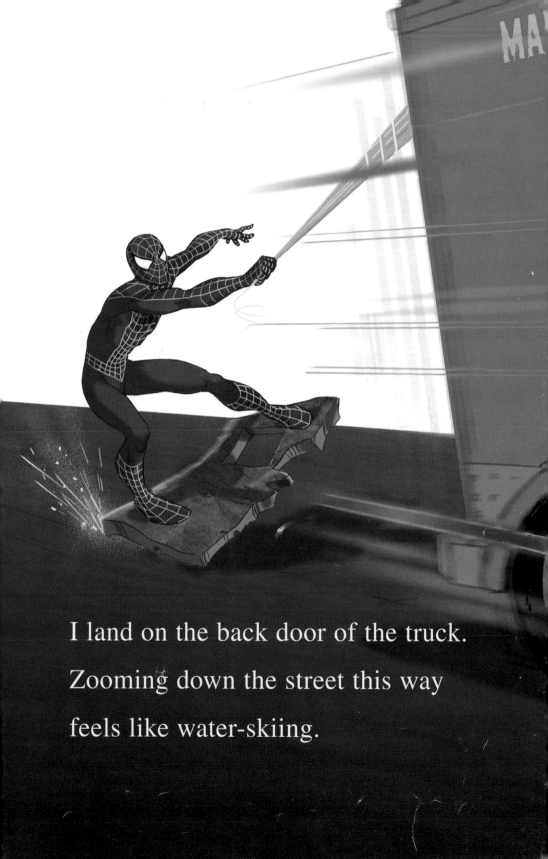

I land on the back door of the truck.
Zooming down the street this way
feels like water-skiing.

I can't let Sandman get away
with that money.
But my job is to protect the people
of this city.

I will do anything to help the people.

That's the most important thing of all.

And little kids need protection
more than anyone.

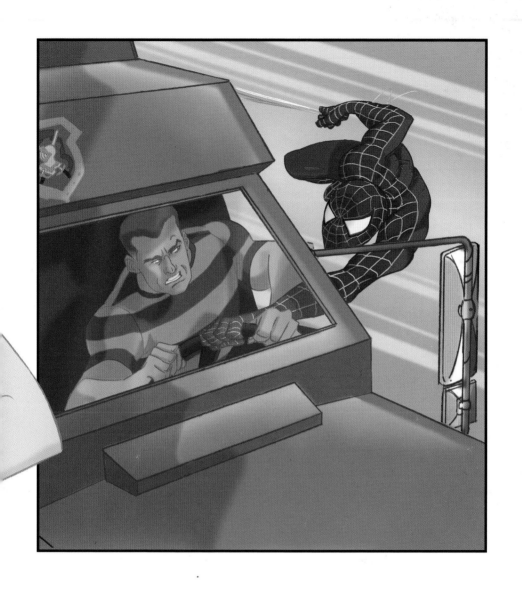

It's time to go to work!

I need to stop Sandman

and get this truck under control.

I'll say good-bye to Sandman for now.

This little girl needs my help.

But I won't let Sandman get away for long.

Helping people is the best part of my job.

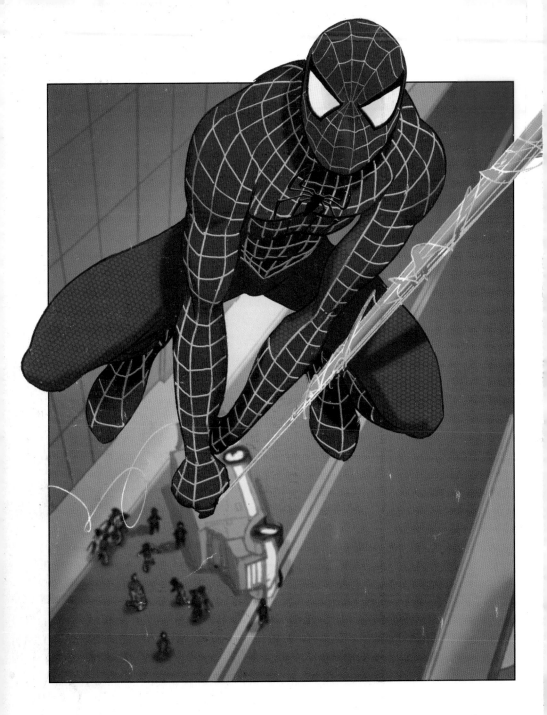

And now it's time to find Sandman!

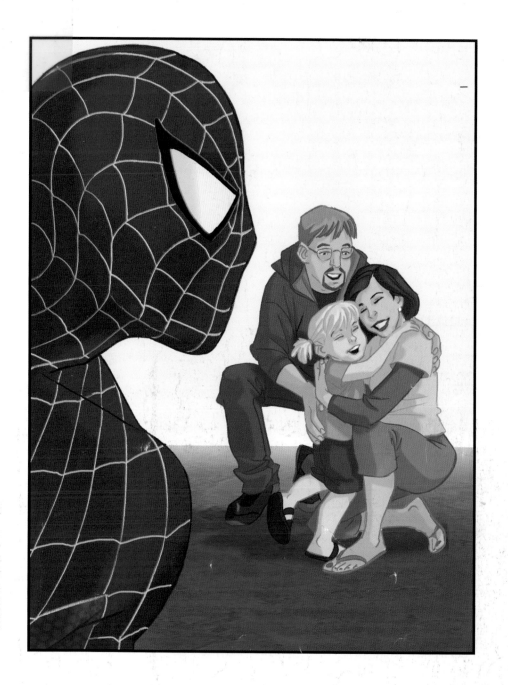

I like to make people happy.